Published by Diggz Ditches ISBN: 9798999125804
Copyright © 2025

For permission, questions or concerns please contact me at diggzditches@gmail.com or (424) 260-3612

Thank you god for showing me your love through the kindness of others, your hope through tribulation and your infinite light through darkness. And thank you to my great aunt for believing in me when I couldn't believe in myself.

DUST

Table of Contents

Dust 1

Spirit 69

ABA SAYS.

Oh Father! Birther of the Cosmos, you create all that moves in light. Focus your light within us – make it useful.

Matthew 6:

Sky 84:5:11

At night, ABA tells stories about an old lonely and cold world, where all life was made of dirt and had a duty to her. But suddenly, as if swallowing a bitter curse, it became broken and greed filled, so overflowing with suffering and cruelty, that now it's long forgotten and never missed. And ABA says that "back before the dirt had shriveled up to dust the skies were so clear that you could see it; sitting there, spinning itself crazy and   eating its own blood. Consumed by its own nothingness. Until one cycle, it stopped spinning. And began spilling its dust into the skies. Filling its depths with purple and pink clouds, impossible to see past."

So now we often find ourselves lost in the thoughts of this vast expanse, staring deeply and pondering at the dust it left behind. An elaborate system of stories told to fancy the mind; the way that dreams are made. The first time we dreamt of this past; we were in our 7th sleep cycle. It felt like watching a forgotten memory, a speck of dust was just crying underneath a dead tree. Its face frozen yet bursting

with an indescribable sadness we had never seen. Dee
cries, shouts, and shrieks erupting from this speck, jus
sitting there where nothing should be. We still dream of
from time to time; not always sad but always crying, alway
so slimy and covered in dirt. ABA says "there isn't a singl
thing down there that isn't dust." And every fish in ou
pond and every fruit from our trees comes from a world tha
once was, just like us. But whenever we close our eyes an
listen deeply, we can hear that speck; moaning in agony
And if we sit still long enough, we can see it sitting there
Where nothing should be, the essence of dreams.

The first time ABA took us to the *Center* of this perfec
realm, we were set FREE. Walking through its walls, our live
transformed into vivid pictures before us, more a mirro
than anything. The *Center* knows all that was and is, bu
only ABA knows what will be. She created the *Center*, that
in turn created our world here in the sky, above the clouds
Far, far away from the dirt, with no bloodshed and no end
We are safe here, where the cosmos can be chased withou
fear. In fact it puzzles us that the dirt, which encompasse
such vast worlds, chose to hurt itself so profoundly

Sometimes, we question how we could come from dirt at all. During the dirt's end, we were filled with awe. As ashes returned to ashes And dust returned to dust, freeing us from that world and its cruelty. Yet, when we dream about that thing down there, where no one should be, it doesn't appear cruel; it seems to be in pain, a hurt that we had never known.

But just a circle ago, as we were hanging with our friends at the center of the Center as we do every 3rd cycle. We fell off the highest part of the climbing tree and hit our head on a large rock. It didn't hurt but, we imagined that the bouncy surface was hard and firm, just like the dirt we had seen that speck crying on. We wept, thinking of it sitting there, lost in so much agony. In an instant, that speck became real to us, alive within us. None of our friends understood that our tears were not for us, but for it. This thing that does not exist. No one could comprehend, when we tried to describe the depth of that pain. So we hurried down the blue-lit halls into the deepest regions of the center to find ABA.

We wanted to tell her what we felt. It's frail an
withered frame enveloping within, eyes bruised, saggin
and filled with sorrow. Hair knotted into grey and blac
braids that hung down to its waist. Having never befo
experienced pain we sought ABA's wisdom. Hoping sh
would know how to mend it or explain the nature of th
speck. But when we finally finished saying all that we had 1
say, ABA just chuckled softly and exclaimed , "you alway
did have such a beautiful ability to imagine." At th
moment, our stomach swelled with embarrassment; We ho
no idea why. She was right; in fact we had spent most o
our lives painting worlds that no longer exist. This pain wc
linked to a being that maybe existed eons ago. Still, w
couldn't help but feel this; Was it all in our head? Th
creature whose pain we could fall into so easily? "Thanks
we muttered as we meandered back up the blue-lit halls t
the recreation room. A wide-open space on the surface o
the center; where we hang, play, and create.

Sophia and Ariel were relaxing on the rocks near th
climbing tree. So we skip across the bouncy floors towarc
the tree to say goodbye and notice the light shining throug

he skies. How it shimmered across Ariel's skin cascading off of the large mirror like shards that formed into a grand, statuesque figure. The   radiant dance of light splintered nto a rainbow of hues across the room; as Ariel sat smiling and sharing laughter with Sophia, who flew up above the ree. A gentle glow of swirling pastels wisped gracefully hrough an aura of joy so high in the sky; never touching the floor.   No none of us ever needed to touch the floor but here was a soothing quality to it, a calming embrace that pulled us into slower movement.   Except for Sophia, who was always floating right past time.

When we arrived we sat for a cycle talking about all hat had happened and then announced that we needed to return home. Sophie, with a familiar spark, reminds us of our plans to attend the antiquated myths summit, but we decide to skip it. We indulged for some time in a lingering embrace, caressing one another tenderly, before slipping away. So that we might come to understand this new dream that lives. Catching the winding track home we arrive at a large wooden cabin, perched majestically within a gentle hill covered in soft and vibrant moss.

As we walk up the pebble path toward the door, w
recall the feelings of that moment; falling off the climbin
tree and subsequently the way that its pain swelled withir
pushing us to become something more or less than th
before. And as we fell asleep we thought of ABA and he
timeless stories, thought about the glory she passe
through dreams of the dirts unbecoming. I expected tho
with reflection, this new sensation would fade away.

Yet today, when ABA asked about our dreams as sh
did every morning, we were engulfed by that sam
menacing heat. Except this time we felt ensnared, th
words swirling like a storm in our head. "We always di
have such a beautiful ability to imagine." A complimen
sure, but it seemed so... out of place. Was it merel
imagination? The pain of this thing, that found itself in th
depths of our flesh.

The words twisted around in our chest, sticking itself t
our throat as ABA asked again; "How did you sleep?" bu
we couldn't speak; the thoughts ran deep, and we couldn'
explain the depth of these feelings. Why did it hurt so much

and why did we crave to sit with this discomfort? As if understanding it would lead to something? We left ABA at the table, nursing her breakfast, and took our hurt to our room. Our hurt, or its hurt. To tell the truth this hurt felt so foreign within our body.

We've only felt hurt, once before this. A fleeting moment when Ariel introduced us to bleeding when we were still teething. Our tears never even reached a full cycle. A teething star and a warm hug was all that was needed to restore us. In our world, hurt didn't linger into pain, so what is this lingering thing? Tonight we will go to Ari's slumber party. Self assured all we needed is music and good friends to lift our spirits. Besides, Sophie loved new experiences. We'll have fun exploring this painful thing together. And Ari is bound to offer sage advice. Nothing is better medicine than friendship.

Sky 84:06:12

We took the winding track at the bottom of the hill. As we walked down the soft moss caressed our toes, while the

firm clay beneath it molded gently with our feet. offering it
security and delicateness. The track's doors opened befor
us, and we took a seat, gazing up at the sequined sky as w
pulled away from the front deck. While cradling the pai
within, we began to converse with it. Asking questions like
"Why are you here? And what is your purpose? What does
mean that we are the one you come to? And who are you
Where do you come from? How are we able to hold ya?
Our thoughts linger on these questions. Staring perplexed c
the clouds, at all the distorted facts of our past. Thought c
all the stories of the dirt's pain, but this bad? It wa
unfathomable. The pain didn't answer, but we sensed it
need to be seen, to be felt. Or like it needed our help. Sc
we held on; and maybe for too long

Finally, we arrived at Ari's slumber party. An oasis c
light shoots through the sky down onto the large bubbl
nestled along the riverbank. The path is led down wit
chrome marble stepping stones. As we walk along the
reveal a network of eyes tracing across our indigo skin wit
glimmering orchid swirls caressing our curves. Our larg
majestic shimmering beige wings, crafted by ABA, remaine

idden within their own magnificent expanse. At that moment, the discomfort left for a while, and feeling worthwhile, a swell of pride fills its place as we enter into the transparent, spherical home of our friend. Inside, a vibrant symphony of music and delectable aromas welcome us.

Within Ari's home, our world is redeemed in its limitlessness. The central console overflowed with a plethora of tiny pies; some sweet, some savory, alongside a bubbling fountain of ginger punch. We congregate here each night to fill the space with joy and light. The evening typically began with joyous dancing and warm idle chatter. Kali, Manitou, Yamantakan, Sophia, Kokopeli , Alekwu and Vidar were having fun dancing with one another, while Ariel, Ngai, Bunjil, and Oden lounged on the couches, deep in conversation and laughter.

As we approached eager to join in the dancing, we found ourself standing there staring into the gleeful expressions. And rather than being swept up with happiness. We felt a strange detachment. Arcane chasm between the joy and the pain enveloping within us. Like the

laughter clashed against the weight of its sorrow, an
hallowly brought forth the red tide of embarrassment. Ang
mingled with sadness, leaving us fragile. We felt a litt
broken, unable to talk, we couldn't find the words to explai
and even if we could, would anyone understand? Peop
don't really get hurt here. How are we hurting here? Whe
we are free from that.

After some time spent grappling with our mind; w
decided to take its hurt, or our hurt, for a walk. We neede
to be alone, which was a feeling we had never known. S
when it came we raised our hand and shouted, "we need
leave now." This sentence met with concerned stares, lov
and a few sorrowful farewells. We began to walk home, n
taking the track back because we needed to think,
soothe ourselves. We needed to breathe. And at the sam
time we have no idea what we need.

On the way,   we passed through the park tha
surrounded the center. The opal path was illuminated wit
soft pink lights, as the stars shine brightly in the sky. W
began to wonder about the clouds, transformed from th

emnants of dirt. The dirt was no longer just dirt, nothing remained but that cloud. Proof that this pain thing, that this connection to this pain, isn't real but somehow that felt like a lie. As we continued through the park, we noticed that many of the trees we passed by were filled with fruits, connected by bridges and surrounded by slides and book nooks. All filled with life and illuminated by lights. But the tree under which the speck stood, looked withered and empty, its bark cracked and breaking. We had never noticed these things before, and that felt real. We spent the next cycle astonished at all that is.

Sky 84: 07: 07

When we arrived home, we walked into the kitchen where ABA sat and rushed past her, waving her away, and exclaimed "We love you," As we made our way toward the backyard, we felt the sweet waters calling to us. Knowing we needed their comfort. As we passed through the threshold toward the base of the hill, we felt the small, round lake near the small oak tree at its bottom beckoning us with each step, the stones perfectly molded to our feet.

Upon reaching the lake, we stared at our reflectio shimmering across the water. We jumped in, and the warr air met the cool water, soothing the pain we carried withi us. We swam over to the waterfall trickling down the hi where the water's energy felt its strongest. We couldn figure out if we wanted to let go of this bond tha connected us, or pull it stronger. We were just so curious an confused. We stood beneath the waterfall, wrestling with th pain and questions for as long as we could manage an when we felt ready, we pulled ourselves out of the lake, an carried its pain within us up the small hill toward the purpl wisteria tree.

Walking up each step is filled with calm and as we si beneath the tree we note the comfort of its shade. Th beauty of this world becomes magnified by these nev sensations. We trace the sensation coursing through ou body with our fingertips. Gently pressing them against ou temples, following the feeling. Lingering our fingers acros the closed eyes, along our neck and shoulders. And dow our arms, and across our chest, until we reached the hur deep into the pit of our stomach, where one of our eyes began to cry.

We pressed our fingertips into the hurt right above the ear. As we reach into that pain, pushing more firmly, more deeply. We feel it tearing into us, opening us up. Our cheeks became hot and wet, as our breathing became labored. Why were we feeling this way? What was happening to us? Our thoughts swirled into a storm. Faster and faster as we lost connection to our world and ourselves.

WHERE AM I?

The kingdom of heaven is like a man who sowed good seed
in his field. But while everyone was sleeping, his enemy
came and sowed weeds among the wheat, and went away.
When the wheat sprouted and formed heads, then the
weeds also appeared.

Matthew 13:2

Unknown 00:00:00

All that remained was air too sharp to breathe and too hot to think. Then, when that was gone, all that was left was darkness and WE were gone. I..I was trapped. When I looked up I saw that there were no stars or sun in sight, just a heavy shroud of thick clouds swirling around me. The ground beneath my hands felt wet and slimy, and as I tried to breathe, I was oppressed by the very air I needed. My vision blurred into a mix of tears and darkness, And as I reached out, desperate to find myself in this fog. My own arm was lost to me, and the weight of everything felt like it was compressing me. Was this a dream? It had to be. But it all felt too real. Too painful. And dark and cold. The dampness clinging to me in a way that words could hardly capture. My nose burned from a putrid smell, and my eyes stung with tears. Everything was hurting, and it felt like too much to bear.

Suddenly, a voice broke through the haze, harsh yet frail. . "Yuh deah." A figure emerged from the swirling clouds, I still struggled to get up, my body trembled under

the weight of fear. "Don't ya know better than nah wa
around all flesh and bone like ya are?" I wanted to respon
but just then it dawned on me; I hadn't taken a real brea
since...The shadow moved closer, and I attempted to ris
once more, but my legs wobbled beneath me, keeping m
tied to the floor. Just then , it appeared to my side, offerir
support "Get on from here, child , for there ain't nothir
left." Its voice is disorientating, nothing but rhythm ar
conviction.It spoke tongue. I wanted to reply, but my voic
was lost.

That is until It wrapped my head in a warm beige clot
and I felt a flicker of relief. It was easier to breathe. But ju
hardly and as we began to flee my feet sting with each co
step. Panic set in when I tripped on something hard ar
wet. "Where am I?" I shouted. My voice echoing off th
fabrics I was wrapped in. Suddenly, I felt a gentle hand c
the back of my neck. "Foolish child," it murmured, pulling n
away faster. "Come now." A numbness washed over n
body "whhh why wud" I managed to stutter through n
tears. "Hush now, hush," it urged, its warmth grounding n
pulling me from the depths of shock.

After what felt like a lifetime of running, I was brought into a large, yet cramped room echoing with many voices. Those voices weren't born of the spirit but burst forth from the tongues of many beings. Yet there was a strange beauty in their chaotic chatter, as if they were all able to understand one another despite all of the noise. As the warm hand left my side and the cloth slipped from my face, I looked up into a sea of faces. There were more beings gathered here than I had ever seen, all in a room smaller than even a closet should be. And the dirt. It was everywhere. On the floors, the walls, the furniture. A tapestry of different kinds of earth.The people surrounding me wore expressions of bewilderment, their faces streaked with grime. Some had extra limbs, while others lacked. The dirt intertwined with everything here.

I had never witnessed such a gathering in one small space. If someone had told me just last cycle that beings could exist without legs or a traditional sense of a soul, I would have been astounded, but now I only felt confusion. The chanting filled my ears, mixing with the weighty air that somehow felt both fresh and dreadful. And then, a figure

appeared before me, tall and thin, carrying the scent c
burnt sweet woods. With trembling eyes, I traced its form i
disbelief. Its ragged blue dress, black-and-grey braids, an
the pain that lingered in its essence made my heart ache.

"It... it's you," I whispered, a faint tremor in my voice
The figure spoke to me in tongues, yet its spirit resonate
within my own. "Help!" it cried out, a plea that ser
shockwaves through my heart. Tears streamed down m
face as I closed my eyes, overwhelmed by confusion an
fear. This can't be real... thoughts raced through my minc
How did I end up here? With these beings? How were the
living, breathing, existing? This dream felt unlike any I'd eve
seen; too vivid, too intense. I felt trapped in a reality fille
with pain and confusion.

My heart pounded against my chest; each beat echoe
the deep distress rising within me. Detached from who
used to be . I couldn't bear to be here, wherever "here" wa
Suddenly, a cold hand wiped away my tears, and in tha
moment, my racing thoughts slowly quieted as I began t
open my eyes.

Sky 84:10:11

"Messika? , please, sika!" we open our eyes and find ABA crouched over us, her expression one of pure concern, lifting our head into her warm lap and supporting our neck with care. A sense of safety enveloped us, the pain fading and the air in our lungs feeling fresh and invigorating. As we lifted our gaze to meet ABAs comforting eyes, we felt lighter, as all the pain and burdens of that dark place faded away. "Are you okay, little one?" she asks, her voice filled with love and reassurance. A bit confused, we rub our eyes and take in our surroundings. We are home, and we feel safe. We are together again. "We are fine," we say, allowing the warmth of those words to sink in. "Great actually." Everything is perfect. We are connected to our pod and breathing fresh air. There's no pain in our body, just a fading memory; the thing dreams are made of.

When we look up at ABA, we notice her confusion. "Great?" she asks, a hint of doubt in her voice. We nod eagerly, before stretching out our arms and cracking our back allowing our wings to spread themselves.   We

understand her skepticism; the last thing we remember wo
overwhelming and well impossible. But in that instant, w
can't bring ourselves to care. The dream has ended, an
next time we will avoid the pain by any measure. All is we
We are home and we feel great. That is, until we see he
trembling slightly, as a tear rolls down her face. "I found yo
underneath the wisteria tree, bleeding from your sacr
eye," she says, each word feeling like it's tearing at he
heart. The same voice she uses when she talks about tha
old world crumbling apart. We have the urge to comfo
her, but before we can rise, ABA sits beside us, laying
gentle hand on our shoulder. She pauses, searching for th
right words; her tear-streaked face revealing how deep
this affects her. That pain has spread through us; into thos
we love most.

"We are so sorry," our voice quivering yet palpabl
pulling her in for a tight hug, wanting to take away th
sorrow. "We are okay. We just fell off that tree and hav
been having this wild dream since ... Well, it all seems s
silly now." She takes a deep breath and asks unconvinced
"The climbing tree?" a nervous laughter bubbles soft

within her, but the worry remains. We nod, feeling a wave of guilt wash over us. "That's all, we swear," we say, wiping her tears away. Part of us believes it, but another part deep in the pit of our stomach knows the truth is more complicated.

Suddenly, ABA stands up with a spark in her eyes. That calls for some hot cocoa!" she exclaims, and we hesitate, torn. "That's okay," we say, "we'll get a bit more rest." It's a lie, of course—hot cocoa sounds wonderful, and we certainly don't need more rest. But the guilt hangs heavy. "You're not done," she teases as she starts to leave, pausing for a response. With a final breath of relief, she smiles at me again. "Well, I love you, little one." we smiled back, our heart warmed. "We love you too, ABA." As we settle back down in our pod we reflect on what has happened.

Sky 85:11:01

We wake up to the comforting smell of home cooked meals, wrapped in warmth and softness. There's no pain, just a gentle echo of a memory. We venture into the kitchen, where ABA beams, surrounded by an array of 15 large

platters of food. "What's all this?" we ask, both bewildere
and thankful. It's been so long since we ate something. No
disconnected from our pod, we feel ravenous, and fir
ourselves devouring french toast with one hand whi
reaching for eggs with the other. ABA chuckles, watchir
with eyes full of warmth.

"I thought you might be hungry," she says. Her gaz
drifts for a moment, reflecting on something weighed dow
by sorrow as she places her arm on our shoulder. "We
anyway, I bet you and food have a lot of catching up
do," she says, her smile returning as she gives us a quid
peck on the cheek before retreating. ABA often seek
comfort in solitude, finding a strong companionship wit
loneliness. As she walks away, we can't help but call oi
playfully, "Wait, you made all this for little old us?" He
response lighthearted, "For whoever," as she playful
stomps off. Seeing her joyful again fills us with happiness.

We call Sophia and Ariel, eager to be together aga
and happily await their presence while reminiscing on ho
long it's been. Ari arrives first, enveloping us in a long hu

"We've missed each other, no? It feels like ages!" We say. And looking instinctively at the kitchen table Ari reaches for a biscuit from the table and exclaims "Wow, praise be to ABA!" "Yes, and we knew just who to call!" "Okay, let us thank her! These biscuits are so fluffy! And is that bits and gravy?" Ariel adds with surprise. "She must've really missed us!" we nod, fully embracing the moment.

"Funny thing is, it only felt like a cycle this time." "The dream? That's wild. I don't think I've even made it past 7 cycles of sleep. And what were we going for 36?" "Technically, 40," we joke, but suddenly the atmosphere dims. The lightheartedness fades, and an uncomfortable silence envelops us. Then, Ari's face drops, and worry begins etching itself into us. "Are we okay?" Ari vocalizes with fear, as if sensing the full weight of what we've experienced.

"Oh yes, yes. Don't worry," we reassure, though part of us knows it's only half true. "It was nice... Well, not nice, but it was something different, something new?" we say, swallowing the rest of the truth, hoping not to slip back into

that place. Deep down, we all know there's somethin
unspoken.

A shadow lingers in the air just as Sophia come
bursting into the room, tears streamed down our faces, o
the door slams itself shut. "Messsiiii!" sopia exclaims "It'
been ages!" we shriek in unison, tossing our bag
haphazardly onto the floor. Rushing towards each other, ou
hearts racing as we clasped hands and gaze longingly int
one another's eyes. A single tear glided down our cheel
and we could see that nothing was the same.
After soaking in the moment, Sophia's voice broke through
stern yet affectionate, leaning in to plant a quick kiss on ou
cheek between each word. "DON'T. EVER. DO. THA
AGAIN," we shouted insistently, brows furrowed in moc
anger. Suddenly, the reality of the situation hits us. "Oh no
The party! We left in such a hurry!" our eyes darted to An
who stood to our left coyly agreeing "Yeah, it wa
perplexing , but as long as we're okay,"

We wrapped our arms around each other in o
comforting embrace, letting the warmth of friendship was

over us. We can't believe we forgot. This precious time slipped through the cracks of our mind. "We are so sorry, Ari. So sorry, Sophia," We stammered, tears brimming in our eyes. Just as we prepared to say more, Sophia impatiently nudged Ari to the side, our energy bursting.

"So, what did we miss? Tell us everything!" We chuckled. Sophia's lively spirit always had a way of lifting our moods. Ari playfully pushed Sophia's arm. "We can discuss all of this over some food," we decided. Then looking around our mouth-watered, as our gaze swept over to the muffins, while quickly reaching for steaming mugs of hot cocoa. "Oh! ABA is the best," Sophia squealed in delight. "Yeah!" we said, pausing to think. "Should we head into the hot spring so that we don't disturb ABA?" "Ooooooooooh! Hot Spring! Hot Spring!" Sophi chanted excitedly. Ari interrupted, tone mocking, "But we don't want to 'disturb' ABA" laughter spilling over as we swallowed our unspoken thoughts.

Sophia's radiant spirit always filled any room. While Ari's had a more buzzing yet steady demeanor. When we

were together the balance made us feel complete. As w
made our way over to the hot spring, our senses wer
electrified by the promise of warmth. Jumping into th
steaming water, eagerly leaning into one another, wantin
to learn more "So, spill it! What happened?" sophi teasec
"Hmmm, where to begin? Well, it was so absolutely an
unbelievably cold" We took a breath as we pondered on th
words. "Imagine living inside a glass of ice water but th
water is dry. Eerily dry. In fact the only thing that wasn
dry was the floor,""Wait so the air was dry but the FLOO
had water on it?!" Sophia asked, shocked. "Not just on th
floor but seeped into it. Like walking on the mud pit bu
inside it were sharp chunks of natter with no purpose but t
slash into feet "

As we recount our chilling adventure, an aura of shoc
envelops us, as if each word spoken transports us back t
that moment. "We felt strange; heavy, almost as if ou
bodies were made of trees. It was like moving through
thick fog. And then, out of nowhere, a tiny pebble cam
rolling towards us and dragged us across the dirt," w
continued. Sophia's eyes widened in disbelief interruptin

Wait we touched it? That doesn't sound right!" "Actually it
.. it helped us," we stammered. Then feeling the weight of
he words. We gasped, half in horror and half in curiosity.
helped us? But how could that be?" Ari joined in, we could
ee that the explanation was beyond us.

So that we might understand, we leaned in closer. "It
came to us, speaking in tongues, we couldn't understand
what it was saying but we felt compelled to follow it. Every
tep was agony, every breath a struggle against the fierce
wind that stung our eyes. Until it draped us in a fabric that
melled strange, allowing us to finally breathe," we
explained very slowly. "But how could you walk if it was so
painful? And how" Ari asked, lost in wonder.

"It felt like our feet had no choice. The temperature
switched from ice cold to scorching hot in an instant,
melting away my sense of reality. All we had was that
minuscule speck of dust pulling us toward the unknown," we
eply. Sophia, processing everything, said, "That's a lot to
unpack. Are we sure this is just a dream?" A thought
bloomed in our head, well it can't be real can it?

"It's curious, isn't it?" Ari added. "We've never dreame
of pain and suffocation before. Maybe we should steer clea
of that place." Sophia nodded in agreement adding "What
we were trapped for an entire dimension? What then
"Honestly, we doubt that's possible, but being alone fo
three circles with nothing but a pod for company felt like a
eternity," we said with a heavy heart. "Anyway, tell us who
we did while I was gone," we said, feeling the weight o
what we'd just shared. Before we could reflect more, Soph
playfully punched our arm.

"Oh, the party we missed? Well after leaving us w
were confused ""Well our mysterious ways, that's no
unusual is it?" We all chuckled for some time before A
chimed in, laughter bubbling up. "That's definitely true!" W
splashed water playfully at one other, continuing t
reminisce. Sophia continued "After a few moments of worr
we sat down to eat, playing a few rounds of dungeons an
dragons, then showered together under the waterfall, befor
drifting off to sleep watching." "Guess which one?" A
chimed in, a gleam in our eye.

We racked our brains for a moment. "Resan? Empire? "Close!" Sophie replied, grinning. "The imitation of Christ!" we giggled at the nostalgia. Our laughter echoed late into the night, until eventually, Ariel then Sophia headed home. That evening was filled with warmth and affection, a deep bond that felt more significant due to the time we spent apart. Embraced once again in each other's presence, we cherished one another. Anticipating change in eternity feels like a rare gift.

It makes us mindful of the precious time we once knew, and we are sometimes cautious as to not become trapped within time. Aba has granted us cycles in place of change, a way to keep us tethered , reminding us that even in this timeless realm, transformation is possible.

WHAT IS REAL?

Today you eat dead things and make them into something
living: but when you will be in the Light, what will you do
then? For then you will become two instead of one; when
you become two, what will you do?

—Thomas 1

Sky 85:11:11

That night, my mind raced with one question. "What if it is real?" Sleep eluded us, but considering all of the rest we had indulged in already figured that was more than ok. So instead we drifted to the bathroom, yearning to cleanse and release ourselves from this questioning. The room wrapped around us   like an embrace; four walls adorned with rich turquoise stone and floors carpeted in soft plume moss.

Walking over to the tub we stared at its soothing waters reflecting the soft candle light above oozing its calm energy into the room. As our figure sways to the tranquil sounds of birds singing in the distance blended with the melodic trickling of water cascading over the unmoving stones that held our home together . And before we knew it, we were floating on the water's surface, inhaling the herbal fragrance that hung in the misty air.

Wrapped in the soothing warmth, we began to drift into a dreamlike state, sinking slowly down deep beneath the water until our head met the soft rocks below. Kelp tha had once rested on the floor of the tub; floated up, swayin gracefully above us before settling softly across our bod wrapping us in a cocoon.

Then, abruptly, a whisper yanked us from the depths c slumber. "If thou shalt know of evil, pluck out thine eyes The waters thickened, clouding around us, and we felt a invisible weight pinning us to the floor of that tub. "For thou shalt see evil, pluck out thy tongue." The voice gre louder, reverberating through our very core , yet its meanin eluded us. What was this evil it spoke of? Who, or what wc addressing us? The disembodied voice surged again. "FO if thou shalt seek evil, pluck out thine hands." Tremor coursed through our body. We tried to scream, but no soun emerged.

It felt as if a storm had been swallowed whole, only t be unleashed upon us in an overwhelming wave culminating in a bellow: "For he who is evil, shall b nothing." Were we evil? Perhaps it was the dirt and tho dream? Or maybe this voice was simply introducing itself?

We struggled to peer deeper into the suffocating darkness, but visibility slipped away like sand through our fingers. Our limbs felt as though they were shackled, and each passing second burdened us more, the very air vibrating like a struck brass gong. Then, as if the room itself remembered its true essence, everything froze.

In the profound darkness, a flicker of light emerged; its warmth offering comfort in stark contrast to the cold void surrounding me. I reached for it, but I lost my grip and fell, the light expanding, pulling me toward its radiant core. In an instant, it loudly proclaimed: "If thou shalt see nothing, say nothing. IF thou shalt say nothing, feel nothing. If thou shalt feel nothing, know nothing. And if you can see nothing, say nothing, feel nothing, and know nothing, you can make nothing evil."

Unknown 00:00:00

The light enveloped me; warm, yet blinding. I could breathe. I could move. I felt as though I could float! I longed to linger in this realm where the air was infused with

the sweetness of wood and lilac, a clarity swimming withi
my thoughts. But where was I? And what the hell was evi
Suddenly, the brilliant light thickened with wisps c
forget-me-nots intertwined with orchids, spilling the
beauty into the space around me I began shrinking dow
to the size of a raindrop, cascading from the edge of
blooming orchid, plunging both swiftly alongside the ligh
and slowly into the embrace of eternity.

Caught between the reality of who I was and what
was becoming, I realized my ignorance of both in what
am. What am I? Gazing into the endless expanse. As th
transformation blossoms into soft rays dancing inside m
Reminding me of my insignificance, when deep in the abys
of light, I spotted a speck of dust, something nev
Something delicate.

Through it I recognized myself; utterly small, aching
fragile, neither bound by a beginning nor an end. Just tw
entities drifting towards one another In the depth c
eternity. As I hovered in that boundless space, I becam
aware of the stillness of the speck. The longer I stared int

ts depths, the more time seemed to stretch. The greater the duration of eternity, the larger the speck feels. And as the speck gained weight, so did I; my essence became heavier.

More impatient, more corporeal, and more in touch with memories of what once was. The dirt morphed into the light within the light. Soon, eternity lost its terrifying edge and transformed into something more vibrant. Given texture, a true richness and profound sense of realness while simultaneously so surreal.

Nazareth 5BC:05:05

The first breath I took sliced through me with unrelenting agony. Not a diluted pain, but a fierce, bone-shattering kind. An intensity that rattled through my very being, igniting a taste of iron in my mouth. Surveying my surroundings, I stare into the abyss as I hear its spirit calling again. "Help!" Its ancient whispers tugging insistently at me. It needed me in ways I couldn't yet comprehend. Yet, amidst the chaos, I felt its dirt or flesh carving itself into me. Mingling me with its darkness, disheartened dance o creation and decay.

Suddenly, I was ripped away from the thing I came fo and thrown into the imperfect water. Teary eyed I criec since it was hurting me "aaeeuhhhhhghya!" I shouted. I responded back in tongue, "Yeshua," then smacked me! Th dirt and its crooked ways.   In response, I shouted in m own tongue, "Waahhh duh gaaaahhh." I needed help, bu my tongue felt slimy and unwieldy, moving excessively There were millions of sounds with a billion meanings, eac representing nothing, conveying a sense of emptiness. Eac tongue seemed to separate itself from its own essence.

After a while, I was returned to the one I had come fo I called out to it and instantly felt its spirit soothe me, it warmth washing over me like a tidal wave. This world wasn just pain; there was a tiny miracle trapped behind the eye of the one from which I came. Why was I so willing to giv up the before for what is? When what is, has until now been fueled by pain, fear, and darkness, and a glimmer of miracle trapped in the torment.

Egypt 2BC: 25:12

Everything moved so quickly here. The one in the blue dress is called Ama, and since coming home, she wears a variety of colors, showcasing a range of emotions. Her spirit cried out to me every time she changed. Her sadness, fear, and anger were all so confusing and new. When she spoke her aramaic, she did so slowly and softly, lingering on each word. I tried to mimic her, but my new tongue, like everything else here, felt heavy and complex, with so many sounds to sort through. I could hardly hold myself up; I needed to be held just to do anything.

It was the closest feeling to what once was: warm, safe, and soft. The one who had ripped me away was there too. Aba mostly wore reds and blues. Its spirit was quieter, always buzzing and muttering about the dirt and itself.

Since joining the dirt, I learned that it was always trying to distinguish itself from itself, creating stories about who it was and was not. It never fully realized itself. Everything here was made from dirt, and that dirt was dead. We slept on remnants of the dead, draped in the skins, and

Ama and Aba legitimately ate the dead. We lived in dea
houses filled with lifeless toys. I couldn't tell if death was
trophy or a toy, but it certainly made up the majority c
what remained.

The light I saw in Ama's eyes was the life that thrive
within death. It lived in the center of the dirt, like wate
giving life to the soil. Here, life itself is a miracle; a brigh
spot in a dismal reality. Home was a tree and a small patc
of yellow grass surrounded by dust, beneath a sky tho
shifted by the hour; a miracle. Each moment stretche
painfully, time feeling both slow and fleeting. Everythin
was always moving, buzzing, spinning. This dead plac
clashed against the light that somehow managed to endur
the wreckage.

Egypt 2BC: 7:09

As time passed, the "before" became less real and fe
more like a fading dream, then a dream of a dream. Th
more I learned about this world filled with death and pair
the less I dreamed, the less I existed. This make-believ

and, which I had chosen over the "before," became more tangible, solid. Eventually, I was able to lift myself up, to pull myself out from within. I could talk, walk, and run. But the more I did, the less I felt capable of truly connecting with my spirit. It was true that I could walk, but could I float?

The more I learned, the less I knew. I was constantly becoming and unbecoming. I could remember nothing from before, except a sense of its existence living within me. But as my mother began reading me stories of the creator I began to know the truth of myself and the nature of the before through the one they call God or Elohim.

WHo AM I?

Your heavenly domain approaches. Let your will come true in the universe, just as on earth. Give us wisdom for our daily needs.

- Matthew 6:

Nazareth 2 AD: 31:12

The first time I had the dream, I had just turned seven. A speck of light was flying through the sky where all things should be. Its brightness shined past the clouds to remind me of what was. I knew of this light before, but here in darkness, I could not see it, until this dream. My ama, the one whose pain brought me here knew of the light, though she couldn't understand it. She thought God was the light, but I knew that wasn't the case. Rather the light was created long before separation. And the center of this light is where divine things exist with no end. Its rays extend themselves into us to reveal the truth. At night before bed my ama would read me the talmud, sacred scrolls written by the generations of peoples grappling with the truth.

This truth was bitter to people filled with evil, so they spit it out. Claiming to see the light but if they could they'd be alive.   But nothing outside of the light survives. Exogenous genesis before wickedness found matter to trap the spirit in. This matter is known as evil; it exists in all

things that divide and destroy. They named me Yeshua o
the day I learned of evil.

Separating me from my flesh as dust separates fron
dust until it was no longer dust but speck. From that day or
I could see the evil that was within them. There was nothing
but darkness continually until the dream. When deep withi
the midst of the darkness, I saw the light and understood it

The laws were created on the day mankind learned o
evil. So that through the purging of sins, the flesh coul
begin healing and one day learn the truth. Many neede
this purging like my aba, he could not see the light; he wa
filled with rage all the time. He, like the others, committe
every sin above and below the law. It wasn't his fault that h
couldn't understand the law or its purpose. In truth, ther
was only one law: Be good and multiply; the law of the light.

A few days after the dream, a child about my ag
bumped into my shoulder, and I could feel the light withi
him begging to return to the before, to be free from the dir
and its death. I touched his arm and returned the light s

hat the one might become two. His body fell to the floor, and dust returned to dust.

The others gathered around me, throwing stones and ying that I had killed him. I hadn't, but they didn't know hat they were dead and not living focused on the finite and unforgiving world. The light I freed waste living within despite the death, which made it alive. The dust was simply becoming itself again. But how could you explain life to someone who never had it? I returned the light to his flesh. I breathed through him and in receiving my breath he was bitter to me. But his parents were relieved and astonished. No one really understood me here. I didn't even understand myself; like a strange and bitter fruit inflicted upon the land.

Nicknamed the truth

THE RULERS PLIGHT.

Then the King will say to those on His right; "Come, you whom my Father has blessed, take your inheritance, the Kingdom prepared for you from the founding of the world"

—Matthew 25:3

Nazareth 3 AD: 31:3

There was a lot about this world that I didn't understand. And because I was, in the before, there was also a lot that only I could understand. Like when my aba took me into the city and we passed by men on crosses; he would curse the world because they were dead. Could he not see that he was just as dead as they were? Or that the man on the right cross was not dead but alive? That he was with the light? It was those who executed them who were trapped here with this dead place. Simplified the reciprocal plague. It was their own darkness that kept them here.

Or when thieves stole some of the stone aba worked with, and he spent two weeks calling upon his God, cursing the thieves. Could he not see that the stone did not matter? It was his cursing that mattered; the cursing that caused the darkness that stole the light. If only he had asked his God to see the light, he might have realized that true wealth was not found in this world, but in the light alone and he might atone for his sins and meet the true god. My ama knew of the light, but she could not feel it. She could picture

it in the skies and in her mind, She understood its natur
but couldn't see that it resided within.

At night, she would tell me stories of God saying, "Wh
are you cast down, O my soul? And why are you disquiete
within me? Hope in Alaha." Could she not see that her so
was cast down only because she could not feel the light?
only she had asked to truly feel it, maybe she might be lifte
up, and truly living. I struggled to understand all of this. Wh
choose death over what lives? Why fight and kill over dea
things when eternal life is offered to anyone who truly seek
it?

The true light of this world was within them. But the
were distracted seeking the light within the reflections of th
dirt. Unfortunately, the light in the dirt was corrupted by th
death it had consumed. While it mirrored the light tha
reflected through God it was not the true light because
was filled with darkness. As such, they used the bones o
their fellow man to build their towers, adorning themselve
with shiny rags. The more they built, the more the
destroyed, convinced they had found the pleasures of Go

If only they would stop searching for pleasures and focus on the treasures within them.

Jerusalem 7 AD: 20:3

I sat with what I couldn't understand for a while, trying to adjust myself to this world. I learned of their rituals and rules, subjecting myself to them. But while the dirt subjected itself to the law, it also manipulated the law to its own will. They couldn't understand the law because they were not very bright. Yet, they only needed the law because they were without the light. They searched for it endlessly because they knew it was desirable. Mistaking its desirability for desire itself, they pursued the things desired; inspired by the inequities of their flesh. They felt alive in their desires, closer to God even, but these desires were not of the light. All their desires stemmed from death because this world itself was dead. Thus, the law was created to destroy desire so that the light might live, even if they could not.

This plight was not of this world but rather it within it. God placed it here within Jerusalem, a fight with no end. So

that the benighted might begin to fight against the thing
that they can't see. And so that the innocent might be free
But no matter how hard I tried to understand this place. A
of its separations, a castrated agnation. trapping itse
within itself, fracturing into shards. I couldn't understan
how deep within the sharpness of those shards, the ligh
perseveres.

Jerusalem 7AD:21:3

I walked to the temple to discuss with the elders abou
the light and all the godly things that radiate from it. Go
put them in charge of the light but they kept it hidder
There was nothing but darkness within them, and the
committed every misdeed, driven by desire that turned int
greed.

Placing themselves on pedestals, spreading thos
detectable lies so the people don't get wise to the ineffabl
nature of the light inside. And destroy what rules them
Instead they made themselves rulers. Created names and
stories to separate themselves from people who they saw a

beneath them. But still it was beautiful how they described t, like a word given without meaning. The word filled them with wonder and sounded delightful to the ears.

They used it to speak of spritely things. Amidst the yelling and laughing, someone would occasionally say something so profound it would cut through the darkness. However, even the guardians of the scrolls, written by thousands of years of experiences with the light; still could not see it and couldn't fathom its unfathomable radiance. If they could, they would not hide it here. What they could imagine, they named Elohim, Alaha, Yahweh, or Jehovah; the Creator.

But they didn't know the creator. And what do they imagine of his creations? Do they know God or not? They weren't his children. For those who rule are children of darkness. There is only one just ruler. I tried to help them out when I went on speaking of the light, of its infinite radiance, it's as if I were speaking another language.

The eldest man, the wisest of the bunch, spent no tim
speaking. But as for the others they went on testi "how ca
you teach these things being the youngest here? To whos
authority do you have to say such odd things? Is this nc
blasphemy? Is this not the child slayer? Is he not demo
possessed?" They charged. And as they did my parent
charged in, to take me away. Stuck in shock and disarra
As the elders began cursing the all. Our sacred bloodline
the treasured connection to the before.

My Ama who had spent every morning preparing m
for this moment went into a haze when it came. Ashame
of what they had to say. She was always searching fc
sadness that way. Searching for ways to heal the madnes
like that. To be alone with it. Searched for loneliness t
search for sadness in. Was so sad about the dirt and it
wars and its famine and so forth. She imagined all sorts c
sad things when it came to me and about this moment. S
when she came she did so angrily, claiming I couldn't ru
off like that. But I reminded her of who I am.

YESHUA'S WALK

Since the error had no root, she was in a fog regarding the father. She was preparing works of forgetfulness and fears in order, by these means, to beguile those of the middle and to make them captive.

-valentinus

Puri 14AD: 7:10

The moment I stepped out of the temple, my dreams o
the light ignited like wildfire. I could almost hear the ca
urging me to embark on a journey toward the radiant ligh
I was so curious as to why the light was not here? That
had to leave the sanctuary of my home to find it. But
learned the earth was a master at preserving itself, usin
the pain of death to hold onto the all, trapping in an etern
cycle of suffering. .

In the beginning, unity thrived within the dirt. Yet on
foggy evening, jealousy reared its ugly head as the di
began to envy the water's vastness. It tore itself apar
giving birth to continents that battled against the ve
essence of the water. Those continents, now fractured an
pained, transformed into tribes hell-bent on destroying th
dirt for what she did. And those tribes, now tattered fron
their battle with matter, became individuals who in the
loneliness began to wrestle with their own nature. And the
spirit, being so wounded, failed to recognize that the ligh
resided within it. That it, like the unyielding waters, wer

alive and blameless, pulsating with energy, yet shrouded in darkness.

When the spirit embraces the light, it can pierce the shadows of even the darkest hearts. But when enslaved by the flesh, one becomes depraved as forgetfulness emerges. The flesh became a puppet, wielded by the dirt, feeding on hunger, pain, and rage. These forces thrive within the flesh, while the light awaits struggling to shine through its disheartened layers. The flesh was only alive because of the light it turned away from. And the spirit knowing this fought relentlessly against the flesh, just as the flesh waged war against itself. As such the people began fragmenting themselves into Roman or Jew, male or female, rich or poor, each annihilating the other, and in turn, themselves.

As I ventured further from God's home in search of the elusive light, I discovered it among people who had never even whispered a single name from those scrolls. It was through God's infinite oneness that this light was born. It was God's gift, paving the way for them to see the luminescence that transcended separation. Those who

dwelled in the light found a vivid oneness, escaping th
chains of division. But how could it be that the light flickere
so dimly in Jerusalem while here, amid the chaos of dirt an
division, it thrived vibrantly? These individuals lacked th
law, yet it didn't matter; they existed amidst separatior
yearning for the light as they withered in its shadow. The
battled for it, spending their lives together, clinging to th
infinite oneness. The moment I stepped my very foot int
the city, an electrifying energy surged around me as peopl
flocked to me, sensing the glow radiating from within. The
adorned me with gifts, calling me Vishnu, spinning tales c
Sophia and Arielle but renaming them Brahma and Shiv
They honored God as Aum, remembering through fairy tale
and such things.

While the people of Jerusalem busied themselves wit
blood sacrifices and noisy prayers, these vibrant soul
turned away from the grotesque offerings of death
choosing instead not to feast on dead things, rathe
sacrificing themselves to the power of life, a quiet type c
prayer. The so-called chosen people clutched the ligh
hiding it within their temples, quietly reading scrolls whil

oudly shouting their prayers. They believed they were protectors, but in truth, they only confined the light, corrupting both it and their own souls in the process.

The people here prayed silently and told stories about the light begging to see it, for you to see it. Painted images of divine things. Things actually close to God. What if the elders had unleashed God's light like this? Perhaps they could see it and not be so blinded by darkness. As I felt that surge of rage and anguish from this world, its palpable unfairness enveloped me, thrusting me back into that tragic place. Just then everything goes dark as thousands of voices begin swirling around me in chaos. Getting louder as a formidable, bone-shaking voice echoes through the chaos, a powerful decree:

"And if you can see nothing, say nothing, feel nothing, and know nothing, you can make nothing evil." This realm of death, this churning rage that divides us, has severed humanity from the truth. This world and its people, lost in the labyrinth of despair. I am not here, where am I?

COMPLETION

We meditate on the Supreme Being, the Creator, whose divine light illuminates all kingdoms physical, mental, and spiritual. May this divine light illuminate our wisdom.

- Gayatri Mantr

Unknown 00:00:00

"Hello, little one. I think it's time for us to have a conversation." As I opened my eyes, I found myself submerged in water, with ABA towering above me. "ABA!" I cried out, as I hurriedly swam into her embrace, letting my emotions flow as I pressed myself against her shoulder. "I'm so sorry," I exclaimed, tears streaming down my face. Wait, I thought to myself; I'm still dust? Still yeshua? and I'm still alive. I looked up at ABA, who was gazing down at me with gentle kindness. She lifted me out of the bath and settled me on her lap. "We don't have much time," she said firmly. "Time?" I echoed, puzzled. "Why would there be a worry about time in this timeless place?" "I am timeless," she explained. "This place is timeless, and eventually, you will be too. But as for now, you must act swiftly. There is so much to do, so much to say. We have all the time and yet none at all."

"ABA should I be afraid?" I asked tentatively. She looked at me thoughtfully. "Yes, in your realm. But as for now, focus on your tasks. First, you must understand this

curse." "Curse?" I repeated, confusion filling my mind. "Ye
my child. Listen closely so you can begin to comprehen
Long before your beginning, I sat here as solitude within
realm of perfection." A chuckle escaped me despite m
confusion. "ABA, I know this story." But she continue
undeterred.

"After an eternity of isolated perfection, in m
loneliness, I created a new realm that existed beyon
myself and my perfect realm. I created imperfection. It wo
beautiful, and I watched in awe as it birthed wonderf
things: time, space, matter. And within my desire to be, wi
imperfection. I created the unknown. So that together w
could create perfectly imperfect entities. Stars, planet
entire worlds that reflected our essence.

But one day, imperfection had a flawed vision an
isolated in its own imperfection, unintentionally create
something else ""The dirt," I interjected, excitemer
bubbling up within me. "Yes, little one," she affirme
"Imperfection did not mean to create the dirt; it arose fro
evil, born through the very place imperfection dwelled

'Evil?" I replied, bewildered.   "Yes. Evil was not like imperfection; it simply existed outside of him. Made up of what was not.

While imperfection can be beautiful, evil was devoid of purpose, it could only seek to destroy. Because it was nothing, nothing could ever satisfy it." "ABA, I'm... I'm so confused." "Just listen, so that when your time comes, you will understand," she said softly, her eyes glistening with tears. "Imperfection is beautiful and creative, but true light originates from the perfect realm. All things outside of me exist as imperfection, which in turn exists from what did not exist until existence did.

" Now that nothingness exists, what will you do?"

Galilee 25 AD: 01: 26

When she finished speaking, I closed my eyes in order to recenter my thoughts. But when I opened them again, she was gone. Leaving only flickers of light shining through a small opening within the stone home I now resided in.

I looked at my aged hands and scanned the room, trying t
remember what I could about this place. But the last fe
years had become a blur. I stood up from the sma
uncomfortable cot where I had been lying, and a wave o
emotions washed over me. Crying, I spotted a vase of wate
and threw it over my head. The breeze attempted to calr
me as I shouted in frustration at all the pain I felt. Memorie
flooded back: I was a carpenter, my father died, I cried,
imprisoned the light, I was imprisoned, I started
revolution, I abandoned my friends, some of my friend
died.

Suddenly, my ama appeared. "My son, it is time." Sh
came to me in the same blue dress she wore in my dream:
wrapped me in white linen, and handed me a cup of water.
drank and bowed to her before heading out to the rive
where Yahanan awaited my presence. "Thank you fo
keeping us safe all these years." She replied smiling as sh
began to pray. As I walked toward the river, I looked at th
life my flesh had made while I was gone. The homes he bui
were full of love. He took rocks; things without life, dea
things, and gave them the power to be filled with life onc

more. He wasn't in the light yet, but soon he would be born again and have another chance at life.

When I arrived at the river where I was to be baptized, I walked over to Yahanan, as a cool breeze came down, pushing me towards the water. As I stepped into it, I felt ABA's spirit descend upon me. I was with her at the beginning, before creation, enveloped in her perfection. It was quiet and serene. My flesh fell away as the fires of her truth ignited, light of the true light, one with ABA. Still. Serene. In an instant, ABA plucked me from her side and threw me outside of herself. Creation emerged from separation.

I stared in astonishment, feeling myself becoming something other than ABA; becoming imperfection. Tears swelled within as I was pushed out into the skies. My breath transforms into winds out of the fear of being without her. I create time and space solely from my desire to see her again. Now I understand what ABA meant.

I saw the world, from creation until now, fold itself int
a single image. You may know him as Yahweh, the crafter o
fairy tales, the matter maker, or brahma. I know us as Arie
my dearest friend.   In the perfect world, imperfectio
cannot exist; it is purged away along with all of it
wickedness. You may know this purging as the holy Spiri
the first breaths of first breaths, the sacred inner baptism o
divine knowledge, or Shiva. I know us as Sophia, m
beloved.

As I gazed out into the world, my eyes were for the firs
time truly open to its beauty, and I found comfort in m
duties. As I watched the sun glimmer on the sea, I felt it
warmth energizing me. I brought Yahanan in for a quic
hug, then hurried to do all that has been spoken of durin
my time.

What is death to an angel?

The first sermon I delivered to the men by the river began
like this:

The light inside grows bright when you know yourself;
a preeminent wealth.
Euphemistically speaking, the fruit you tended in your
garden.
With withered roots too tender to take stalk in.
The door was closed, yet you heard knocking.
Non-myopic logic starts knocking you from yourself.
While counting sheep, you dreamed he found you.
Lost a piece of yourself.
And discovered a peace you could get lost in. ALAHA!

These men just want to see you cry for the sake of their
suffering. They don't want to see you shine; they say your
brightness is smothering. The truth is, these men are afraid
of the light. They claim that greatness is nothing because
demons only come out at night, prefer the darkness they
covet.'

Anyway, what are you coming with?
When God comes for what's his, what will you show Him?

Life is short. No time for nothingness;
No naughty time for knuckleheads
who don't understand what nothing is.
When nothingness comes knocking, do you have the
knowledge to stop the darkness from coming in?
Yes, I know you possess knowledge,
But what have you learned from sin?
And yes, I know God is your father; don't be a bastard kid
Be like Lazarus; be glad you're His.
His love heals all, so fill up your glasses.
If you want to be perfect, just give up everything and follow
Him. Swallow your fear, and you'll realize that trauma just
gets in the way when you don't acknowledge it
God can clear up all of it! Just follow Him!
Seek the truth of eternal kindness; and He'll help you cure
your spiritual blindness.

68

And thus my last sermon went as this:

So that God may know you, know God.

God is good.
Everything created by God is good.
Everything that exists is created by God

SPIRIT

Here is a list of triggers that came into my spirit

Oppression

Marginalization

Child abuse

Death

Sensory trauma related to the flesh

This new flesh.

Unite our will to yours, so that we can walk with authority as with every creature and Create in me a divine cooperation, from many selves, one voice, one action

Matthew 6:10

U.S. 09: 12: 25

When I was young, my father would tell stories abou
the perfect realm. Where unicorns and fairies lived far up i
the skies. And had a party every night. And everyone wa
invited. I would stare up in excitement as he said this. He'
smile exclaiming this world lived within us. From the leave
on every tree and the stripes on every bumblebee. A
illuminated by its gentle light shining through the skie
where anything was possible. But around here, we don
believe in fairy tales. We know the difference betwee
dreams and what's real. Because dreams don't last lon
around here. People who dream big find that they won't las
here. So we learn not to dream. Because deep in realit
things bleed. But in this world of tragedy, bleeding isn't th
worst of all tragedies.

The first time my dreams turned dark, I was seve
years old. It all began with a smell; A rotting, wretched sme
that made you feel trapped in a shell of what once wa
Safety, peace, happiness; all shattered like broken glass o
the floor. Accompanied by the sweet, lingering stench of to

much whiskey and smoke, of warm, damp breaths, a leaky faucet, excessive sweat, and decaying flesh. In this darkness, where all of them unicorns and fairies can't save you. Here, where things breathe and bleed, and even God can't save you. When prayers become little more than wishes to a world that no longer exists. This is where evil lives.

J.S 10: 09:07.

I woke up this morning the same way I do every morning: sweaty and more tired than when I started. I stepped out onto the warm, soft carpet carefully. Trying my best not to wake my mother, who shared a wall with me. The soft carpet creaked softly under my feet as I pushed myself up tiredly. I quietly slinked over to the large, cracked wooden door, putting most of my weight on the tips of my toes. As I cracked the door open gently, I listened intently. "Nnnn Kukhkhukh." My body released tension at the sound, and I began to fall into myself. My breath returns softly as a ight, damp breeze seeps through the cracked kitchen window and brushes against my face. My feet fall heavier

onto the warm carpet as I take a deep breath. Befor
stepping out onto the cold black and white laminate floor.
tingle slips down my spine. I am electric. My ears perk up o
the silent, crisp air. As I quietly slide my feet across the floo
toward the bathroom. I feel a gulp swell in my throa
knowing that if my mother hears me, she might awake
from her sleep and see me walking around barefoot o
these floors, which may make her roar. This fear didn
entice me because I am electric. I feel the cold, brisk a
charging my skin, sending surges of energy down my spine
By the time I reach the shower I will be at my prime, but b
the time the water has warmed I will be a shaking an
slobbering mess. This knowledge won't deter me from th
quest; as I have already said I am electric.

When I reach the bathroom, I am in full glory. M
breathing quickened, and energy poured through me. At th
moment, even pain would be worth it. Then it struck m
that I had forgotten my clothes, realizing the path had spl
into two roads. I could either shower, get the floor wet, ris
slipping, and incur her wrath, or I could get my clothes an
quickly run back, hoping to return before the water

warmed. I pressed my ear against the door, listened for the sounds of my mother, and knew whatever I chose could get me in trouble.

I looked at my feet, decided to avoid the puddle, and quickly ran back to my room, hoping she wouldn't see me. "Morning, Ma!" I exclaimed just as I closed my door. "Mmmhmmm," she responded, already aware of my antics. "Dion, you know better than that. Put on those damn house shoes " she yelled. I complied; throwing my clothes over my shoulder slipping into my shoes. Every day, a new problem brought me back to you. You never yelled about shoes.

My daddy is gone now, but when he was around
He was my light
Sacred brightness and the wise eyes I confided in
Like back when I was 6
Looking up at the moons disparted nature in anguish sayin
"It's surrounded by so much darkness."
that's when he taught this:

"Trust your fears and nightmares;
they show you where your heart is."

That's when I knew I was an artist.
My daddy was a storyteller; a drug dealer,
And I never had to worry about
where his heart is or starving.

But now, my daddy's heart is in the ground.
He left behind a crown that's too heavy for me to carry.
Alone and lost in a world that's suddenly scary.
And burdened with all this heartache
and rage from watching my heart break;
They got him with a shot to the head.
How could I feel safe?
How good them pills taste, chasing away pain
Degrading your name because normal no longer feels okay
This sin is prized to pay, so you can't really test my faith.

I've seen the darkness
Beaten often for being soft and young
and old enough to catch a stray

swing from a tree branch hitting my back
that tingles when the breeze attacks it.
Acting like normal to feel this pain;
feel like it's healthy to feel this shame.

As I showered I scrubbed myself vigorously; hoping to push all of these feelings down. But as I go out walking through the town. I begin wondering; how long is this road that I'm walking down? I'm new to town, my mama is always moving around. I wonder where she will leave me now that my daddy's not around? On my way to class I try to ignore the piles of trash. There's a homeless man beside the trash, and I toss him some cash. He grunts disgustedly, but well adjusted to who I am, I say, "God bless you" and carry on. I know this world tends to hate me. Saying things that are untrue or misconstrued on the day we learned what evil is.

Before i ever make it to class they enter my path so tha
they might condemn me saying   I'll never meet Jesu
because:

I am a Broke, Black, Queer, Disabled person.
In other words, everybody has got their purpose.
From the football player to the theater kid;
A classic tale of got and get
What does it mean to be perfect?
And can you defeat the curses that hunt you at night?
And when your mama leaves you,
crying and needing, and bleeding on these streets.
How much are you really worth then?
I'm a broke, black, queer, disabled person.
Not everyone has found their worth through others' sins.
Trapped somewhere between
the bottom of your shoe and the floor of this barrel.
And I know that I'm too soft but I can't afford to fight it.
I know my kindness might save my life after it's gone..
And that all of these labels used to separate us,
Blinded by disconnection; you just can't see us because
We are a broke, black, queer, disabled person.

As this group surrounds me, I too condemn them saying:

"You're a destructively rugged, morally pungent person.
Your soul is abhorrent!
Defeated because your demons stay lurking.
Wearing the mark of Cain,
you remain continually slaying hearts.
You never played your part;
Sinning has left you sitting in hell.
Wondering why your roots have rebuked you
when filthy suits you so well.
Your pockets stay swell!
You're slick; you're flipping, tricking,
you sell your soul to the highest bidder
and just like bitter fruit, you fritter in hell."

"Man, you know how it is in these streets. Gotta get it just like you gotta eat. You either run these streets or these streets run you. Now run those pockets."

You think you run the world?
The truth is you are hardly running yourself.

Controlled by fear and led by greed.
Look at what that's done to your health.
It's got you stressing, and those aren't blessings
they're just worldly possessions pressing down hard,
Connecting you to the wreckage. Wrecking the people up
Dust to dust, you sit in the rubble,
jumbling words and fumbling your soul, never confessing
to the one who forgives and gives you his mercy
You'd rather take down the worthy
just to feel that fleeting glory you're obsessed with."

"Man, forget glory. In these streets, it's either murk or ge
murked, my 'guy' And if the blood's gonna spill regardless,
might as well come out on top."

"What's glory without honor? What are you with no father?
Flushing poison into the ocean? What is life without water
You're tearing the earth apart, raising hell;
It couldn't get hotter to be in charge of suffering.
They say there's fun in this slaughter.
They started the war but we fought it,
Then they taught us the targets to aim at.

Taught you your neighbors to blame.
They're really resourceful that way.
Both of you just love claiming things you didn't create.
God gave us this life. How dare you treat me this way?
God gave us life; how dare you try to take it away?"

"Man, forget all of that with your soft behind. Give me that! Matter of fact (sounds of someone being beaten) We need to eat, man, and you won't last around here long anyway. God doesn't love your soft self anyway. Just be happy you're not dead."

Ok but I'll ask you this question: what is death to an angel?

Unknown 00:00:00

As I soared into the sky, I watched as spirits passed me by, escaping from the confines of the imperfect realm. I knew things were as they should not be. Imperfection lifted me into his left hand, and I realized it was not yet my time and so that we might have more, I asked him again, "Father, have I sinned?" To which he replied:

"You are the thing that made the sin a sin;
a blessing that's been corrupted.
God sent them their one and only, they dogged him out;
Now they're lonely.
As for your flesh, it dealt in crooked ways that blocked you
holy.
Insecure now your bread is moldy.
Greed left your flesh dirty
Cursing to God, as if you haven't committed ten sins
since this morning.
You're not loving your neighbor
instead, you judge and condemn, calling them unholy
worried about their path to holiness while neglecting you
own soul.

"But we were meant for more than just feeling sore and
spending more at silly stores that steal the souls of innocen
children begging to see their mothers more; imprisoning
people for picking flowers, just so they can pick you
vegetables"
Yeah you gather on the streets, flipping off your authority

What is death to an angel?

Claiming: 'nobody has got any authority over me'
Shouting: "God is my master, and in His name shall we all be
free."
But when he came
Did you wash the feet of that homeless man?
Or just let him in when he asked to use your bathroom?
The truth is in this world of sinners,
everything gets tainted.
Darkness changes everything it touches.
As long as you judge and condemn sin, you'll only
condemn yourself.
By following the path of Christ and finding the light within;
dampened as it may be.
Maybe you can find a way to shine it onto this dark world.
There are many paths to this light
because it exists within us all.
But you prayed to God for a rock
like he hadn't made every mountain
Prayed to God like a lot, but mostly begging,
not repenting more like chasing a clock.
Never grew up; life cracked your cup,
and then you gave up.

Children went hungry, hospitals burning,
but you prayed for a rock.
Now think about it , they prayed to God for some socks.
And if we're counting, they pray to God like a lot.
Mostly begging for repentance,
screaming turn off them bombs
Knowing they'll never get their limbs back.
So they just pray that it stops,
Just begging for some food yet on the news
It's like they're banging Allah.
A man with many names, but they say it as if their God's
not your God.
Y'all both be praying a lot. Just keep praying

Besides, Jesus spoke Aramaic and referred to God a
"Alaha". It's simply a rendition of "Elohim." None of thes
names are true names revealed to you upon your return, bu
it is through these names that we will be set free, so yo
may return. Who cares which name sets you free?

Yes, you are praying like Lot,
But what are you doing?

How are you moving? Do you move how you talk?
Or do you let the pain of the world tear your spirit apart?
Are you cruel when cruelty comes to you so you won't
appear soft?
With jagged edges where your heart should be,
you abandoned your God
and become the worst this world has taught you.
When will you start loving your neighbor, like the Savior
taught you?

And when you're asked to wash the feet of a homeless man
or just let him in when he asks to use your bathroom.
Remember that in this world of sinners, we all get tainted
And darkness changes everything it touches.
When given the chance to forgo the pleasures of the flesh
to find the treasures of the soul,
Remember that flesh dies, but the spirit lives on and on;
Whether in torment or bliss; flesh dies but the spirit lives on
and on.

This new world.

Hope deferred makes the heart sick, but a longing fulfilled i

a tree of life

Proverbs 13:1

U.S. 11: 03: 03

This was the third time that my spirit left my flesh to die, and every single time it comes back here, I am crying, scared, and missing what was. And in that time, what had happened was my mother lied and then exorcised me. My room was dirty. I was dirty. She sacrificed me and shortly left me alone again, with no way to connect with my friends. And in that time, I've had many visions, transitioning myself to a mirror of the thing I kept buried beneath the bleeding I sacrificed each week. This isn't the first time I came back bleeding but it was the first time I bled at my right hand. A steady hand calling back to me. Begging me to return to this vessel. But while it was sweet and needed me, more than anything, it just needed to feel. This time around I found myself lying on the ground with a couple of slits on my wrist and a couple pills in my fist.

This time, I found myself walking down the brown, water drenched concrete that felt like L.A. but smelled too much like care for anyone to mistake it as such. The starry eyed moon was mine to clutch. Like a belly full of laughter in the dark night trying to illuminate this harsh life. Trying to remember a time when everything wasn't so different; a time when "separate" just meant spread apart, not angry and distant. When "equal" wasn't a punchline. When breathing wasn't so hard through a broken rib cage, ripped wind chimes.

In L.A, most people are different, like harsh laughter. Ten miles down, most people are different like harsh undertones. Neither has grown to know that being different is the only thing humans excel at. Would rather attach in hate! An aliteral syndicate joined together in ending man. And if you ask me it's taxing to see the dividend when none of this shh adds up. But you were different like soft laughter and soft under tones. , but with me, you were different like falling tears. We were invested in laughing too much, like sore abdomens, and went belligerent how we were talking so loud about the indifference to all of our sameness. Would rather consistently diminish like shade to make those around you more or less than. Why have we become so different? And why am I so afraid to hold your hand, my beloved? Why am I so afraid to hold your hand?

What is death to an angel?

When I awoke from this nightmare, I carried all of this new fear, with this new me, to my new school. Where I didn't have to worry so much about this new flesh. But when I went to lunch and ate alone, carrying all the pain I had, they started with the soft groans, then threw at me their judgment and stares, filling my eyes with tears. Not for myself, but for them. Because I knew that if I hadn't bled, I might be free to carry the hatred and pain they were carrying. But instead, I carried my own, holding onto pain that, in truth, doesn't belong to me.

U.S. 11: 07: 07

Carrying all of this pain inside made me so desperate to see the light so when she ignited like fires burning my flesh away I saw her face and realized that years through darkness had led me astray. There was a war to fight and no time to waste .

Now I be fighting for demons, leading mankind to evil.
Hoping to give them something new to believe in.
And sin isn't something you see or eat.

It shan't be CONSUMED
It's produced like doom and gloom attached to the roots.
EVIL conclusions you construe.
It's true, the big shots may call you cool.
When you're outchea' nick-nacking loot,
knocking out naughty knuckleheads' tooths,
spit spattin' pig latin, or racketeering and steering folks
wrong.
But ask yourself;

Will there be truth or just a lie on your tomb?
If you don't fashion the perfect vessel
the devil will pack up your bones
The kettle will call the pot to cook you up,
And you won't return .

I'm ready for WAR; I'm ready to FIGHT.
I walk with the LORD, so I walk with the LIGHT.
I'm not STRESSING my BLESSINGS.
I know HE stays TESTING ME.
I'm READY for the LESSONS that come in the NIGHT;
He retrained my SIGHT.

Oh lord, if you're walking with GOD
What are those guns for?
I'm just sharing my piece, but the peace is within me.
I've got nothing to fear with Jesus homie.
I'm hoping you see it too.

So I'm asking you:

What is death to an angel?
None of us are safe from the grave, but consider this angle.
None of us are safe in this life.
this SHH is just a dream
So what's sacrifice? None of this is great to a god you see.
I mean, there's nothing here to see.
Swear for everything, this shhh is just make believe.
All of this comes straight from the heart, focus on the love
Everything else sets us apart. Focus on what's good.
Nothing is real except the good
We've forgotten our strength.
Forget all the bull and the crud. Most of us are fake.
forging a world based on fear, spreading what we hate .
You can fight wars without love, but you're sure to lose

What is death to an angel?

When you hate me, you hate you.
Your hate, your evil, and your pain are mine too.
I have as much love for you as I do for myself.
I know the light inside you is just screaming for help,
that the pain of this world has convinced you that hell
is much better than the alternative.
Because the drugs keep you numb
and the hate keeps you warm.
You made money from your masters,
so you can't stand the poor.
Saying "forget the world because life is short"
A delusional lie that keeps you trapped in the dirt.
You've made a king of yourselves and led his people astray
then sat in the pews like a flea in the hay.
You monopolized GOD and robbed his children
but you'll claim it's much better this way.
I tell you this truth , knocking you to your grave;
repent for your ways or get lost in the flames
Get right with GOD, and your soul will be saved.

US 11: 07:20

Relearn your softness.
Let the light shine through the darkness.
As hard as it is to hold on to kindness,
I'd rather risk my life than to try
To let go of that tendency to seek some tender peace.
The most genuine energy
comes from a dark and broken healing
A scary yet hopeful feeling
Like drug dealing or stealing clothes off of factory racks
Trying to rack up a lot of money just so I could get back

The war is not over; it's just another wave.
Can't breathe in forever; at some point you have to let go

And you can return that coffin,
Tossed between rocks as the tide comes in,
breaking bones to fit in.
One might atone for their sins and be grinning
while sinners are sitting and spinning the truth saying:

"Whoty Who was wit da crew when he got blood on his shh"
Them heroes ouchea catching naps;
Now you have blood on your wrist.
Your mama heard your cry for help;
she got your blood on her fist.
Now I choose water over blood, because blood just isn't .

But isn't it curious how greedy hands create more than just
pain?

They took away hope, your dreams, and your faith claiming

*"The war's not over; it's just another wave.
Can't breathe in forever; at some point, you have to let go."*

Tragedy breeds travesties.
Broken anatomy mixed with a little PTSD.
My future is hard to see, or hard to think about
when I remember what you meant to me
or what they did to me while you were gone.

I didn't think I'd make it to 17; I guess that I was wrong.

God got me through it because I wasn't strong.
That's due to my heart, rest in peace to your cartilage
and broken bones. And when you're on your way home
Trapped between rocks as waves tear away at your flesh;

Remember learning that softness is a lesson
You carry till death tears you apart

Dirt 3000:30:03

The ocean stood over me, whispering sweet gifts of orchid and forget-me-nots, tunes of calm bouncing off of a mos pit of a person. Trying to rust away the razor blades I lai on my skin and made with my tongue. Sought to soothe th rumbling belly of the beast I call home. But I have neve known of a place called peace, never seemed to sit properl when faced with the fluttering wreckage of time. I hav never felt so small, never quite so insignificant. But alas that was the true door to peace; humility, the last steppin stone to salvation. But I'd never known of peace like this. S when it came, I was afraid; I cried, feeling for the first tim the fullness of the wreckage of time. I swore to never sit s close to peace again, because unlike fire, bones, and pai peace never cared for the lies I told or the shame. It onl cared for the truth. There's a reason the ocean tastes jus like tears. So I pray on the day I die, when my life crashe down like waves I can be just soft enough for the tides o truth to take me away.

What is evil?

This is the manifestation of the Father and his revelation to his Aeons. He revealed his hidden self and explained it. For who is it who exists if it is not the Father himself? All the spaces are his emanations.

- Gospel of Truth

Unknown: 00:00:00

Once upon a time, deep beneath the skies, lived a curiou
young boy named Seth. On the day Seth was born, he, lik
all other specks, entered into a contract to defeat evil. Th
contract represents the first breath and one might return t
it during the rebirth brought down by the Savior. Now in
hidden truth, the evil that you specks are meant to defea
does not actually exist. Now that this truth has bee
revealed, some will ask, "How can something that does no
exist be defeated?"   Others will ponder, "Why woul
something that does not exist need to be defeated?"

To answer these questions, I ask that you consider this;

Think of yourself standing at the feet of a giganti
mountain. The largest and tallest mountain you   ca
possibly imagine. Now, what if I told you that up at the to
of that mountain, God planted the tree of life and if you at
from it , you would never die. With excitement you migh
begin gathering up everything that you need to climb u
that mountain with glee. But after an hour of climbing yo

begin to watch in agony as ten similarly sized mountains begin merging into itself. But if you are filled with desire or curiosity you might continue climbing. And begin prancing gallantly as fallacy transforms this perspicacity to scanty stagnancy as this mountain doubles its own size. Then triples its mass. And just for good measure, it doubles itself again and again.

 And as you go on climbing or driving or holding onto the enormity of your situation, the weight, the pressure. You realize that no matter how great this weight may feel, and no matter how high you'd convince yourself to climb, you would be no closer to that infinite place than if you had never climbed at all. No, not even a pebble of a step. This truth embodies evil, and its power lies in death and all sinful things. In a way, this non-existence existed before existence did. But in another way, it could not have. How could there be a "before" if "before" had not existed?

For example, imagine one day you wake up and discover you have traveled to the year 20 of the Lord near Bethlehem. You step out, dazed, wanting to go home, and head out towards your fellow man, saying, "I need a car to get home." This sentence is now devoid of meaning, as cars do not exist. This non-existence preceded the very creation of cars, and even if his creations could drive over the vast waters that separate you, they could not help you get home. On the other hand, if you continued searching for Christ and found him, and asked him about this car, He would know and be known, and you might even return. In this way, evil is also known.

Now, in a sense, Seth, the first son of mankind, was the very first person to defeat evil. But in another way, nothing could defeat evil except THE ALL. Some believe that Christ came to defeat evil, but if that were the case, evil would already be defeated. In truth, he was only returning what Seth had taken up. Furthermore, only the speck that can manifest evil can defeat it. For example, how could a God defeat what had not been created? And how could anything exist if it were not created? If you are created and exist, why do you cower before what does not exist?

To the one who believes there is no creator and that nothingness precipitates what is: how then can anything matter? Does matter precipitate itself or not? Consider what is. If THE ALL that is does not reside in the eternal realm, it is found in matter. We know that nothingness cannot create, for it was not created; indeed, it is not. How can nothingness precipitate THE ALL? Is that not where divine things reign? Understand that THE ALL that is has been created by what is. This reflects the true face of God, and its power lies in life and everything that precipitates life. Now, to the one who believes that they are, merely matter: why have you not perfected yourselves and joined us in the perfect realm? If you are matter, real, and alive, why do you kill, suffer and die within her? If it is true that you are a child of matter, why don't you continue living as matter? Who are you? It is true in a way that THE ALL is here with you, but in another sense: why do you suffer and cause suffering? In truth, we are within THE ALL, and THE ALL, is within you. But if you were fully within THE ALL, evil would be torn away and you would see who you are.

You may also wonder, if you are wise, if God is the great precipitator, what precipitates God? I tell you, those who search for the end will find it and may conquer it. And those who conquer it will surely find God.

Now, to the believer who, in truth, does not believe or is blinded by their own belief: I tell you, the non-believer who comes to belief will be more powerful than this one. The non-believer who comes to believe will face punishment from the world for spreading truth, while the believer who spreads lies will be loved by this world but despised by their own beliefs. This is the face of the false believer.

The believer who truly believes may take their gifts away, but the non-believer who actively seeks truth will neither keep their gifts nor have them taken away. This is the face of the true non-believer. In their disbelief, they will seek; if they continue searching, they will be in awe, and their gift will be upon them. Bringing them joy as they delight at THE ALL that precipitates. This is the power of the true non-believer. It cannot be taken away nor kept; it perseveres until the end so that the end can be defeated.

And now, to the one who hates the creator and asks, "How can all of this be created by something good? Has evil not overwhelmed THE ALL?" And has evil not caused suffering? I ask you, how can you hate what has not yet reached you? When the entirety of existence comes to you and washes away your hatred, you will see where it belongs. You may then destroy what has plagued you and return to THE ALL. In doing so, you will know the true love of THE ALL. Until that moment arrives, search for it within those who love and strive to defeat evil; they are the true children of the light.

Now, regarding the children of darkness, whether believers or non-believers. Those of you who do not seek to defeat evil, but rather, you embody it. THE ALL cannot exist as matter because it perishes and does not return. When you die, you will not return. However, you exist, which means you can begin to detach yourself from matter. This is the power of the laws of Moses.

The child of light does not require these laws because the light is not confined to matter; rather, matter exists outside of them. The law of the light is the law of Seth: "Be fruitful

and multiply." Or, as amplified by Christ, "You shall love th
Lord your God with all of your soul . And love your neighbc
as yourself." The fruit of God hears this law, understands i
and does the will of the one who sent them. This is the lav
of the good fruit, and those who partake in it will surel
return to life.

The children of darkness are different, they can nc
understand this law, or pretend not to. They cannot return t
THE ALL because they are outside of what's within then
However, by destroying what is material, they may begin t
live and not merely exist. The law of Moses was establishe
like fires that consume matter. This law is not spiritua
rather, it is of the flesh. Flesh is, as matter, that has bee
softened to seduce the spirit. When one is born, this flesh i
a perfect vessel that surrenders itself . If one does nc
surrender to the spirit that lives within them, they will b
consumed and cast away and will not return. This is the fac
of Moses and his power is in the law. The law is akin t
medicine. Those who are sick seek a cure, and those wh
are healed seek the sick.

Thus, when reading the law, be like a just doctor. If you wake up with a cold, you would not want a doctor who hands you glasses and claims they will cure your cold. Similarly, if you have cold medicine, you wouldn't inspire a blind person by saying, "This medicine can cure you." That is like the law of the light. In contrast, the law of the flesh is the law of darkness, in which one must take what is theirs and destroy what is also theirs.

For example, when a child is born, as all are, it loves the spirit and naturally surrenders to it because it is pleasing. However, let's say this flesh experiences hunger due to the sickness infecting the matter around it, if this is left unchecked, it can harden within the flesh, turning into greed, crushing the spirit and disconnecting it from THE ALL. As the child gazes at their world, they cannot see THE ALL; instead, they see hunger and the matter that provides food. This fruit is bitter because it is material and not alive. After consuming it, one does not go on living. The greedy must fast and surrender to THE ALL, so that they might live.

Now, consider someone beaten with a stick who becomes enraged because their flesh is bruised and brutalized. Matter produced both the stick and their suffering, and their rage is crafted with the law so they may return. The enraged must rest and surrender to THE ALL.

Or, for example, someone who has been humiliated. Enduring stones thrown at them, insulted as "nothing" or "disturbing" Matter does not create this void, nor is it created but it does feast on your hopelessness. Instead, use the law of ABA to transform humiliation into humility so you can return to THE ALL and be exalted.

One who submits to the law dominates the self. One who submits to the self dominates the spirit. And one who submits to the spirit becomes one with THE ALL. Some may ask, Is it not the female who submits to the male? Others may say is it the male who dominates the female?

But I disregard this discourse because it was written at the beginning: ABA says, "Let us make mankind in our image after our likeness"

Thus, your God, Yahweh, who is within all images of God; "created mankind in His own image; in the image of God created He him; male and female created He them." These truths were revealed to you, yet you did not understand them. I reiterate the one who submits also dominates, and the one who dominates also submits.

But what of the one who neither submits nor dominates?
The Savior!
This one is the sacred lamb.
And his sacrifice is the fruit of THE ALL